DATE DUE			

FIC PUR $23.99

Purkiss, Sue.

Ghost school /

32455104000375
CPS- Moos Elementary School
1711 N California Ave
Chicago, IL 60647

GHOST SCHOOL

by S. Purkiss

illustrated by Lynne Chapman

Librarian Reviewer
Kathleen Baxter
Children's Literature Consultant
formerly with Anoka County Library, MN
BA College of Saint Catherine, St. Paul, MN
MA in Library Science, University of Minnesota

Reading Consultant
Elizabeth Stedem
Educator/Consultant, Colorado Springs, CO
MA in Elementary Education, University of Denver, CO

STONE ARCH BOOKS
Minneapolis San Diego

First published in the United States in 2007
by Stone Arch Books,
151 Good Counsel Drive, P.O. Box 669,
Mankato, Minnesota 56002.
www.stonearchbooks.com

Originally published in Great Britain in 2003
by A & C Black Publishers Ltd,
38 Soho Square, London, W1D 3HB.

Library of Congress Cataloging-in-Publication Data
Purkiss, Sue.
    [Spook School]
    Ghost School / by S. Purkiss; illustrated by Lynne Chapman.
    p. cm. — (Pathway Books)
    Originally published under title: Spook School.
    Summary: Although he is supposed to be learning to scare people, a
young ghost who attends the Anne Boleyn Secondary School discovers a
different way to haunt humans.
    ISBN-13: 978-1-59889-114-0 (hardcover)
    ISBN-10: 1-59889-114-6 (hardcover)
    ISBN-13: 978-1-59889-256-7 (paperback
    ISBN-10: 1-59889-256-8 (paperback)
    [1. Ghosts—Fiction. 2. Schools—Fiction. 3. England—Fiction.] I.
Chapman, Lynne, 1960–, ill. II. Title. III. Series.
PZ7.P976513Ghs 2007
[Fic]—dc22   2006005081

Art Director: Heather Kindseth
Graphic Designer: Kay Fraser

1 2 3 4 5 6 11 10 09 08 07 06

Printed in the United States of America.

TABLE OF CONTENTS

"In all my years of teaching, alive and dead, I have never, ever, seen this. One ghost in this class has scored a zero on every single test. I repeat, on every single test. And that ghost is—"

"Nooooooo!" shrieked Spooker Batt, sitting straight up in bed.

His mother appeared beside him. "Goodness, dear, what is it? Did you have a bad dream?"

< 5 >

"The worst," groaned Spooker. "I dreamed that I failed every one of my tests, and Sir Rupert was making fun of me in front of the whole class. It was horrible! He did that thing with his eyeballs, where he gets mad and they stick out more and more, and then they pop out and roll down his face."

"You mustn't worry about the tests," Mrs. Batt said. "Dreams don't always come true. You've been doing fine in most of your classes."

"Yes," said Spooker, "but not Practical Haunting. Sir Rupert really doesn't like me. He shouts, and then I get all confused, and then I make a mess of things, and then he gets even madder, and then—"

"Sir Rupert doesn't like anyone," said his mother.

< 6 >

"It's not in his nature to like people. But there's no point worrying about it. Come on, it's getting dark. You might as well get up." She bustled off to wake the rest of the family up.

Spooker sighed. The trouble was, Sir Rupert's class, Practical Haunting, was the most important one. After all, what good was a ghost who couldn't get out there and haunt? If he failed Practical Haunting, he'd have to repeat the year, and that would be terrible!

"Phanta, hurry up!" called Mrs. Batt. "Spooker's tests start today. We really can't be late."

"I'm never late!" said Phanta. "He's the one who's still in bed." Phanta was Spooker's little sister. Like many little sisters, she was a perfect delight to her parents and a perfect pain to her brother.

< 7 >

She even kept her room clean, which seemed scary to Spooker. Her parents called her Little Blossom, but as far as Spooker was concerned, she was the Evil Weed.

Spooker gave up. He couldn't stay in bed and hide, so he walked downstairs.

His father smiled at him. "You look a little green," he said. "Cheer up. How long do the tests go on for?"

< 8 >

"It's just Haunting History and Ghost Computers tonight. We've already had Dream Weaving and Fright Studies. And then it's three nights for Practical Haunting. I suppose you were really good at tests, Dad," said Spooker.

"I don't think anybody likes tests," said his father. "The important thing is to stay calm. Don't panic, that's what you must remember."

"Don't panic," repeated Spooker, trying to get it into his head. "Don't panic, don't panic."

"Panic? Who's panicking?" demanded Mrs. Batt. "I'll be panicking soon if you don't get a move on, Spooker. Do you have extra pens? And your books?"

"Oops." Spooker realized he'd left them on his desk upstairs.

"I'm ready," said the Weed.

< 9 >

She would be, thought Spooker. She did everything right, and she made sure the people knew about it. No chance she'd ever fail any of her tests. Spooker went up to get his books, and then stuffed them into his book bag.

"Come on, you two. Get a move on," called Mrs. Batt. "Bye. Have a nice night!"

What a joke, thought Spooker. With Practical Haunting as his first class, there was about as much chance of him having a nice night as there was of Sir Rupert turning up with a friendly smile, a kind word, and a gift for each of his students.

< 10 >

CHAPTER 2

Spooker was in Sir Rupert's classroom, sitting to one side and hoping that Sir Rupert wouldn't notice him there. He knew that teachers picked on people in either the front or the back row.

Sir Rupert swept in, wearing his usual velvet clothes and carrying his sword at his side. He believed in tradition and liked wearing clanking chains and a suit of armor. He felt that was the kind of thing people expected ghosts to wear.

< 11 >

But armor and chains were too noisy for school, especially since he liked to creep up quietly and surprise students, and the staff, for that matter. He enjoyed taking his head off and leaving it on the desk to stare at the class, while the rest of him stepped out to find someone else to scare.

"Now," he said, "as you know, you've got tests coming up. I'm expecting good results, and what I expect, I usually get. Isn't that right, Little Bo Peep?"

Little Bo Peep's real name was Holly. She was very quiet and shy. Spooker thought that must be why Sir Rupert picked on her. He didn't approve of any gentleness or niceness.

"Yes," she said, so nervous that she began to fade.

"Yes what?" said the teacher.

< 12 >

"Yes, Sir Rupert, sir," said Holly.

"We're going to review some things today," said Sir Rupert, "so there'll be no excuse for anyone to make a mess of things."

"Not even you," he said, staring at Spooker, who jumped nervously. "Take notes and review them the day before your test. Do whatever you have to do. But remember this: the In-specters are going to be paying us a visit."

Spooker sighed.

When things were bad, you could always be sure they'd get worse.

The In-specters had been introduced a few years ago. The School Board had decided that haunting classes were getting worse. The classes weren't working!

< 13 >

People just didn't seem to be scared of ghosts anymore. Instead of screaming with terror and turning white, people these days just looked interested and pulled out a camera. The School Board decided it was all the fault of the schools, so they formed the In-specter Squads. They were paid lots of money to inspect the schools and make sure they were working.

If there was one thing that was sure to spook the spook teachers, it was the threat of a visit from the In-specters.

Spooker's Aunt Jane was a teacher, and he'd once heard her explaining to his mother why teachers got so nervous about being inspected.

"It's so much work, for one thing," she'd said. "You have to write down plans for every lesson, and make goals, and things like that."

< 14 >

"And you have to be able to prove that you're good at getting your students through tests," she added. "Honestly, it's awful when In-specters come. They're just suddenly there at the back of the class with a clipboard, taking notes on everything you say and do. It's enough to give you a nervous breakdown."

Spooker had a nasty feeling that the In-specters would make things even worse for the students. If Sir Rupert was under pressure about tests, he would know exactly who to take it out on.

Then Spooker realized that everyone was looking at him. He turned around to see where Sir Rupert was. The teacher's voice boomed out behind him.

"When you're ready, Spooker!"

Spooker sat up straight.

< 15 >

Sir Rupert cleared his throat. "Now then, Practical Haunting. Aims — that's what the In-specters like, so that's what we'll give them. What are the aims of Practical Haunting? You there, Little Bo Peep."

Holly trembled. "Um, to remind people about things that happened in a place long ago," she said. "Usually bad things, or sad things, or . . ."

"Yes? Or what?" asked Sir Rupert.

"Um . . . ," said Holly.

"Sir! Sir!" said someone else. "Someone who died for love, sir!"

"Yes, love," said Sir Rupert. "Yes, that can be part of it, but only a very small part. What are the other aims? Anybody?"

"To scare people, sir?" tried Spooker's friend Goof.

< 16 >

"Now that's more like it!" said Sir. Rupert. "Yes, that's what we want to do. Some people say you should try to do some good when you're haunting, try to make some kind of point."

"Well, let me tell you!" Sir Rupert stared at them all, his eyes gleaming like hot coals. "I want to see people running out of haunted buildings, screaming their hearts out, with their hair standing on end. That's what'll get you the top grades."

< 17 >

"Now, I want each of you to write down three Terrifying Tips. Keep them simple. You've got two minutes," said Sir Rupert.

This was easy enough, thought Spooker. Planning how to scare people was all right. He just didn't like doing it. He thought for a while, and then wrote:

1. Turn all the lights off.

2. Make the room freezing cold.

3. Change into something really scary.

When their time was up, Sir Rupert snapped, "Spooker! Go on. Amaze me!"

Spooker read what he'd written.

"Hmm. Well, yes, that's all right, as far as it goes," said his teacher.

"Let's think about the hard part now. What can you make people see that'll really have them sucking their thumb and calling for Mommy?"

< 18 >

"A head cut off!" said someone.

"Hood over the face!"

"Skulls with glowing coals for eyes!"

"Not bad," said Sir Rupert. "A bit easy, but not bad. All right. Any questions?"

Spooker couldn't help wondering, and then suddenly he heard himself speaking out loud. "Sir, do you think it's cruel to make people so scared?" Spooker asked.

The whole class gasped.

Sir Rupert stared at him. "I don't believe I'm hearing this. Of course it's cruel! It's supposed to be! You're a ghost!"

Luckily, the bell rang for break.

"Remember," said Sir Rupert, as everyone left the room, "I'm the one who's doing the grading, so I'm the one you've got to please." He glared at Spooker.

< 19 >

"Don't let me down," said Sir Rupert. "If you don't do something scary, you'll be staying behind a year, and then I'll have another chance to get it into your head. That's all."

With a final look at Spooker, he swept out of the room.

Scary? Spooker groaned. The scariest thing he'd ever made was a ghostly baby owl, cute and fluffy.

What was he going to do?

< 20 >

CHAPTER 3

In the staff room a few minutes later, the principal looked at the teachers. He wasn't sure how they were going to cope with a visit from the In-specters. He didn't feel very hopeful.

"As you know, the In-specters are going to pay us a visit. They may appear at any time. I have the greatest faith in every single one of you," he said, crossing his fingers. "I know you will try your best, and I know just how good that best is."

< 21 >

Sir Rupert snorted. "They'll know a top teacher when they see one." But he didn't look very confident.

The only person who seemed calm was the Ghost Computer teacher, Ged Goole. He was the newest member of the staff, and also the best organized.

"If there's anything I can do to help," he said, "just say the word."

"Thank you, Ged, thank you," the principal said, watching the rest of his staff as each, in their own way, started to panic. "But I'm afraid it'll take more than computers to get us through this safe and sound."

* * *

During break time, Goof and Spooker went out into the playground.

< 22 >

< 23 >

It was a beautiful night, and some of the younger students were playing Throughball in the silvery light of the moon. The Weed was on one of the teams. As Spooker watched, she faked to the left, and then whooshed with a burst of speed to send the ball in a completely different direction. It went straight through a member of the other team. The Weed punched the air with her hand and yelled "Throughball! Yes!" and her team cheered.

'"Look at her," said Spooker. "She's good at everything."

"You're good at stuff too," said Goof. "You're okay at Haunting History, aren't you? You're good at remembering things. Better than I am. And what about Dream Weaving? You got extra credit for your last report, the one about Scrooge."

< 24 >

Dream Weaving and Ghost Computer were both taught by Ged Goole. Dream Weaving wasn't one of the most important classes, but Spooker really enjoyed it. He really liked the story Ged told them of the haunting of Ebenezer Scrooge.

"It's about a greedy old man," Mr. Goole had said. "One Christmas, he has three dreams. The first reminds him of the Christmases he had when he was young and happy. The second shows him the kind of man he has become. And the third shows what will happen in the future, if he doesn't do something about it. He's so scared that he changes his ways. It's an interesting idea, isn't it?"

Their homework had been to plan a series of dreams like the ones in the story, this time for a bully instead of a miser.

< 25 >

Mr. Goole hadn't said how old the bully had to be, and Spooker found himself thinking about Sir Rupert. It had been fun, and a bit of a challenge, to imagine Sir Rupert as a child. In his homework, Spooker had to disguise him, of course, but that was easy. He just turned him into a math teacher and gave him a head that wasn't removable, a shabby jacket with pens in the pocket, and a shirt and tie.

"Yes, I enjoyed doing that," Spooker said. "Much more interesting than skulls and chains and screeches."

Just then, a screech announced the end of break.

Goof made a face.

"Oh well," he said. "That's it. Time to go in."

* * *

< 26 >

The first test was Haunting History, and even though it was one of his best subjects, Spooker still felt nervous as he sat down.

The desks had all been moved as far apart as possible so that no one could cheat. Each desk had a test paper on it. It made the room seem odd and unfamiliar. Even their teacher, the Vanishing Lady, looked a little nervous.

"You have an hour and a half," she said. "Remember to read the paper carefully. If an In-specter should appear, just try not to let it bother you."

Spooker looked at the paper. He remembered his father saying, "Don't panic." He took a deep breath.

The first part of the test was about royal hauntings.

< 27 >

He had to give three examples, describing and explaining the reasons for each haunting. This was good. He had spent a lot of time studying this topic.

For the second part of the test, he had to choose a famous animal haunting and write about it. Animal hauntings were Spooker's favorite.

He thought about the ghostly cat that haunts King John's Hunting Lodge in Somerset, but decided that it wasn't really interesting enough. All it did was walk through closed doors, curl up, go to sleep, and disappear. Instead, he wrote about the White Horse of Uffington.

Spooker was writing about how the horse comes to life once every hundred years. Suddenly he had the feeling that he was being watched.

< 28 >

Spooker looked up.

A pair of glowing eyes was floating around the classroom. Other ghosts had noticed them too, and there was a little ripple of noise. The Vanishing Lady looked up.

"Oh! Is it . . . ?Are you one of the . . .?" Then she began to look angry.

"Wait a minute. I recognize those eyes! Sir Rupert, this is extremely rude of you! You're interrupting my test," said the Lady.

"So sorry," he said. '"Just dropped in to remind everybody of something."

"What?" asked the Lady.

"That my eyes are upon you!"

He howled with laughter as his eyes bounced from one student to another.

< 29 >

* * *

Spooker's final test was after midnight. It was Ghost Computer with Mr. Goole. The test was in the computer room, so it didn't seem like an ordinary test.

"Go into the folder named Test," said Mr. Goole. "You'll see a picture of a castle. Take a look at it, and then write down your ideas for three different hauntings for that castle."

The computer screen showed a picture of an old castle. Spooker clicked in each room, and up popped a little box with a story about what had happened in it.

It was just like playing a game, but Spooker soon realized there was a lot to do to finish the test.

At the end, when they logged off, Mr. Goole smiled at them.

< 30 >

"That wasn't too bad, was it? It looked to me as if you were coming up with some interesting new ideas. Not too many old skeletons and clanking chains."

"What's wrong with clanking chains?" said Sir Rupert, appearing suddenly next to Mr. Goole.

Mr. Goole looked coolly at him.

"They're fine as long as they stay in the history books," he said, "but I think we can do something more modern in the twenty-first century. Don't you, Sir Rupert?"

"Modern? New?" sputtered Sir Rupert. "I'll give you modern, you young . . ."

The principal appeared in between them. "Is everything all right?" he asked politely. "There's someone here I'd like you to meet."

< 31 >

A figure appeared suddenly beside him. It was a man wearing a black suit and holding a clipboard as if it were a deadly weapon. His eyes were colder than a blizzard in Alaska.

"May I introduce the Chief In-specter?" said the principal.

< 32 >

CHAPTER 4

"And then Sir Rupert got quiet," said Spooker with a chuckle. It was just before bedtime, and he was telling his mother how the tests had gone. "It was really funny, Mom, but nobody laughed because of the Chief In-specter being there."

"Will you check my homework, Mommy?" asked the Weed sweetly. She was thinking it was time she reminded everybody how wonderful she was.

< 33 >

"I've spent three hours on it, and it's not even due till next week," she said.

"Well done, dear. This looks terrific." Mrs. Batt smiled at her, and then turned back to Spooker. "Are you sure you've got everything ready for going away?" she asked him.

For Practical Haunting, Spooker's class had to stay away from home. You needed at least three nights for a really good haunting, you had to build it up slowly. So the first night, maybe you'd just make a drop in temperature. The second night, you might add ghostly noises or mysterious lights.

Then on the third night, you'd let loose with the big ending, such as ghostly figures, furniture flying through the air, and whatever else was needed.

< 34 >

Mrs. Batt was looking through
Spooker's bag. "I've packed some spare
clothes and your sleeping bag. I wonder
if there's anything I've forgotten? I hate
to think of you going off all by yourself.
Who knows where you'll end up? Or what
kind of people you'll be with?"

< 35 >

"Now, now," said Mr. Batt. "Don't get the boy all worked up. He'll be fine."

"How do you know?" she demanded. "Things have changed since we were at school. People don't have the respect for ghosts that they used to. What if he comes up against someone who's seen that awful film? What was it called? *Ghostbusters*, that was it. You know, where they had ghost hunters with terrible weapons."

Spooker stared at her.

"That was a story. Pure fantasy. Don't take any notice, Spooks," said Mr. Batt. "Your mother's just worried because it's the first time you've been away by yourself. You'll have a great time, I know you will. With luck, you'll have a nice old mansion to haunt. Creaky doors, echoing corridors, hidden rooms."

< 36 >

"I got the Tower of London for my last Practical Haunting test," he added. "It was wonderful. There was just so much to choose from. Headless queens, bloody ghosts. Oh, it was such fun. I loved every minute." He smiled, remembering.

But Spooker knew that Sir Rupert wouldn't make it that easy. The Tower of London was a dream assignment. It was the kind someone like Sir Rupert would only give to his favorite student.

Not to someone like Spooker.

"I suppose you're right," said Mrs. Batt. "And anyway, the teachers will be there, keeping an eye on him."

Was that supposed to cheer him up?

"I think I'll go up to bed and read through my notes again," said Spooker.

< 37 >

His mother looked cheerful. "Oh no, you won't. You'll go straight to sleep and get a good day's rest. Who knows how much sleep you'll get over the next few days?"

* * *

The day after his talk with the principal and the Chief In-specter, Sir Rupert was also feeling a little worried.

He kept moving his head around his neck, and turning it nervously from side to side.

"Now he knows what it feels like to be graded," whispered Spooker to Goof.

"Your instructions are on the desks in front of you," Sir Rupert said. "You've each been given a different location, and your, um, aim is to carry out the best haunting you can."

< 38 >

"What you're really after," he added, "is to drive the humans out. It takes a lot of skill to do that, so I don't suppose any of you will achieve it."

A clipboard appeared in the air. A pen marked a large X.

Sir Rupert jumped. "What I mean is, I know that you'll all do your very, very best. Remember, to avoid any cheating, you must stay at your site. Myself or one of the other teachers will check on you to make sure you're all right." He tried to smile kindly at them. It was a horrible sight.

"All right then," he said. "Look at your instructions, and then whoosh off as soon as you're ready."

Nervously, Spooker looked at his piece of paper. It said:

< 39 >

> *Go to:*
>
> 6 Buttercup Avenue Hookbridge
>
> Your targets are the Roper Family:
>
> Cyril, Sandra, and Ben

6 Buttercup Avenue?

That didn't sound like a nice old mansion where people would be expecting to see ghosts. It sounded new and clean, and without cellars, old paintings, or any scary feeling at all.

If Spooker had a heart, it would have sunk at this point. He glanced around. Everyone else was already gone.

Sir Rupert was watching him.

"What are you waiting for?" Sir Rupert said. "Go on!"

< 40 >

"Oh, and, Spooker" the teacher added with an evil smile.

"Yes, sir?" asked Spooker.

"Enjoy!"

< 41 >

CHAPTER 5

Soon, Spooker was floating over Hookbridge. It was a small town. Most of the houses were hundreds of years old. He felt that this was a place with lots of ghostly activity. Ghosts would be walking through doors, drifting up staircases, and acting out scenes from the past.

Spooker was surprised. This wasn't what he expected. Maybe it wasn't going to be so bad after all.

< 42 >

He began to feel better. Perhaps Sir Rupert was getting nicer.

Spooker whizzed around, looking at street names. High Street, Church Lane, Silver Street. Where was Buttercup Avenue? He whizzed up higher to get a better view.

Then he saw it. A group of big houses that were so new that some of them were still being built. It was even worse than he expected. In fact, it was probably about as bad as it could be.

Sir Rupert had given Spooker the almost impossible task of haunting a brand-new house, a place that could have no history and no memories.

Spooker sighed, slid silently through a wall, and began to look around.

Every room looked like a picture in a magazine.

< 43 >

There were expensive lamps, white walls, beautiful vases with nothing in them except twigs, designer storage closets, and no mess.

Except one room.

It was a bedroom, and it wasn't tidy at all. In fact, it made Spooker feel homesick, because it reminded him of his own room.

It looked as if the owner was someone who didn't believe in throwing things away. There were clothes all over the floor, and the shelves were crammed with books.

The owner of the room seemed to be interested in wizards. There were two large posters, and each had a wizard on it, along with several other strange-looking people.

Spooker was disappointed to see that there were no pictures of ghosts.

< 44 >

The cleanest part of the room was the desk, which had a computer on it.

The room had a comfortable feel that the rest of the house did not. Spooker started thinking that he would probably like the owner. He gave himself a little shake. Liking people wouldn't be much help when it came to haunting them.

< 45 >

He had to plan. He had to show himself to the Ropers. He had to frighten them, whether he wanted to or not.

But where should he start? Usually when you went into a house, you got all sorts of feelings, little shivers bringing messages from the past. But this house had nothing. It was cold. The only room where he felt comfortable was this one.

There was a big, squashy cushion in a corner, and Spooker lay down on it to relax and try to come up with an idea. He had to get up early that evening, and he was tired. He'd just have a little rest, just close his eyes for a minute.

* * *

When Spooker woke up, a boy was curled up in the bed reading a book, and Mrs. Roper had just come in.

< 46 >

"What's that you're reading, Ben?"
she asked.

"Oh, nothing," said Ben.

"Of course it's something. It's a book,"
she said sharply. "Let me see."

She looked at the cover, and then turned
it over to see what it said on the back.

< 47 >

"I can't understand why you like all this stuff about wizards and vampires and ghosts and werewolves. It's such trash. Why don't you read about real things, like sports?" She handed it back in disgust.

"I don't like sports," said Ben.

"Well, I still think you could find something better than all those silly computer games you waste your time on. It's no wonder you're not doing very well at school." With that, she turned the light out and left.

Spooker felt sorry for Ben. It hadn't seemed a very nice way to say goodnight. He wondered if Ben had a teacher like Sir Rupert at school. Maybe that was the real reason he wasn't doing very well.

Thinking of Sir Rupert reminded Spooker that he wasn't getting very far.

Spooker had to make a plan.

< 48 >

Time was ticking away, and he only had three nights to make an impact. He knew he should try to look at it as a challenge, but somehow he just felt sad.

He sighed, and told himself to think of an idea.

Mrs. Roper certainly didn't seem very sensitive. So whatever Spooker did would have to be very clear. To please Sir Rupert, it would have to be very scary. Perhaps he should concentrate on what he was good at. He was good at animals. He needed a big, scary animal. He tried to remember Sir Rupert's lessons about the use of animals in haunting.

"Dogs are the only choice for a good haunting," the teacher had said. "Make them big, make them mean, make them scary. And don't forget the glowing eyes. That's the part that freaks people out!"

< 49 >

CHAPTER 6

It was dark outside, and Ben was asleep. Spooker went downstairs to see what Ben's parents were up to. They were in the living room, talking.

"I worry about Ben," Mrs. Roper was saying. "He got Cs on his last report card. I think he should be working harder."

"Yes, it's odd, isn't it?" said Mr. Roper. "He doesn't seem to have been born with our brains at all. I don't know what we're going to do with him."

< 50 >

"When I was his age, I was already studying the origin of the universe," added Mr. Roper. "I wasn't messing around reading stories.""

"And I was making fun ways of solving math problems," said Mrs. Roper.

"Children just aren't what they were," said Mr. Roper. "Oh well. I must read this file tonight. Honestly, some people think they can get away with anything. This guy owes us a lot of money. He says he wants more time to pay, just because he's gone out of business."

"I hope you're not going to give in," said his wife.

"You know me better than that, my love. He'll have to sell his house. In fact," Mr. Roper said, chuckling, "he'll probably have to sell his children!"

< 51 >

Spooker was horrified.

What an unpleasant man, and his wife seemed just as bad. Spooker felt much better about doing a really nasty haunting now. In fact, he was looking forward to it. The Ropers deserved all they were going to get.

He went back into Ben's room, where it was quiet and dark and felt friendly, and he thought hard.

He wanted to scare Mr. and Mrs. Roper, but not Ben. With such awful parents and problems at school, Ben had enough to put up with already.

It shouldn't be too difficult to scare just Mr. and Mrs. Roper, Spooker thought. Ben could easily be left out of it.

Spooker figured out what he had to do. Before long, he was ready to start.

< 52 >

First, he would build up the spookiness with an unexplained cold breeze, doors opening and shutting mysteriously, lights going on and off, the usual kinds of things. Then, when the Ropers were starting to get worried, he might try a Ghostly Voice.

Ghost animals sometimes told the future, so the voice could warn of something unpleasant that was about to happen.

A Ghostly Voice was tricky, though. You had to be careful not to overdo it, or it could just sound silly.

The most difficult part would be appearing as the scary dog. Spooker thought he'd leave that till the next night, after he'd had some rest.

"Okay," he said to himself, "time to get on with it."

< 53 >

He went into the Ropers' bedroom and immediately started task number one. The Big Freeze!

Starting just under the ceiling in one corner of the room, Spooker whooshed very fast backward and forward. He kept going back and forth, moving a little further down each time. When a ghost whooshes, it leaves a trail of cold air behind it. Spooker was making layer after layer of icy coldness.

The Ropers began to move in their sleep. The further Spooker came down, the colder the room became. Soon, Mr. Roper was trying to pull the covers off Mrs. Roper. Still half-asleep, she tugged it back again.

The colder it got, the more each of them wanted to keep hold of the covers. Soon, they were fighting each other.

< 54 >

It was so funny to watch that Spooker got the giggles and could hardly keep whooshing. Finally, they both woke up.

"Give me back the blanket! I'm freezing!" said Mrs. Roper.

"You're the one who keeps hogging it! Look, I'm shivering!" said her husband.

"All right. That's your half, and this is my half," she said.

< 55 >

They pulled the blanket right up to their chins, but of course that didn't do them any good because the room was colder than a polar bear's fridge.

"Cyril," said Mrs. Roper through chattering teeth, "why is it so cold?"

Ah! thought Spooker. This is it. Any minute now she's going to realize there's something weird going on!

"Must be that cold front they mentioned on the weather," Mr. Roper said. "I can't understand why it's so cold inside the house. I'll make a fuss about this. I didn't pay for a house that can't keep the cold out. I'll be on the phone first thing tomorrow. I won't put up with this."

Mrs. Roper sighed. "I'm sure you won't, dear." She got out of bed and plodded to the closet to get more blankets. Soon they were snoring again.

< 56 >

Spooker was disappointed. They'd been angry, but they hadn't been afraid. And neither of them thought that there was anything supernatural about the sudden freeze. Spooker didn't think they were very smart. He was going to have to do something even scarier. He decided to do some tricks with the lights.

It was very easy to use his ghostly energy to play with electricity. Spooker soon had the lights in the bedroom flashing on and off, and the Ropers were awake again.

"Now what?" groaned Mrs. Roper.

Mr. Roper got out of bed and pressed the light switch.

Nothing happened.

"This is terrible!" said Mr. Roper. "There's something wrong with the lights, too. Heads are going to roll for this."

< 57 >

"Never mind that," snapped Mrs. Roper. "What are you going to do about it now?"

"What's happening?" asked a sleepy voice quietly.

Ben had been awakened by all the shouting. Spooker quickly switched his spectral energy off. He hadn't meant to disturb Ben.

Suddenly, a familiar voice snarled in Spooker's ear. "What are you stopping for? Lost your nerve, have you?"

Spooker jumped. "No, sir! Sorry, sir!"

"Well, see that you don't! Remember, an In-specter could turn up anywhere, even on Buttercup Avenue. So don't think you're not being watched. I'm leaving now, but I'll be back!"

"That's just great," muttered Spooker, as Sir Rupert faded away.

< 58 >

Spooker decided not to try the Ghostly Voice. The Ropers were making so much noise they probably wouldn't hear the voice anyway. It was getting late and Spooker was tired.

* * *

Ben was looking curiously at the spot where Spooker was standing.

"It's very cold in here, isn't it?" he said, still looking hard. "Much colder than in my room."

His parents paid no attention to him. But that was nothing new, and Ben wasn't thinking about it at the moment. He couldn't think about anything except the boy who was standing in his parents' bedroom. It would have been strange enough for any boy to be there, but there was more to it than that. Because this wasn't a real boy.

< 59 >

No real boy was pale and silvery like that. Even if Ben hadn't read all those ghost stories, he'd have known instantly that this boy was a ghost. A ghost at 6 Buttercup Avenue!

He went back into his own room, chuckling. This was not the kind of thing his parents expected to have as part of their expensive, new home! Awesome!

Soon after, the ghost slipped through the wall and sat down on the floor cushion. This didn't seem to Ben the way that ghosts were supposed to behave.

"Aren't you going to disappear in a clap of thunder or something?" he asked.

The ghost leaped up. "What did you just say?"

"I said—" started Ben.

"No, I mean can you see me?"

< 60 >

"Yes," said Ben, "of course I can. I wouldn't be talking to you otherwise, would I?"

"But you shouldn't be able to," said Spooker. "Why do things always have to go wrong?"

Ben tried to cheer him up.

< 61 >

"I thought it was funny, what you did in Mom and Dad's bedroom, with the cold and the lights. Are you going to do anything else?"

"Um, yes," stammered Spooker. "Well, that's the plan, anyway."

"So you won't be going anywhere?"

"No. Not yet, anyway," said Spooker.

"Good," said Ben sleepily. "It's nice, having somebody to talk to."

Spooker felt wide awake. People weren't supposed to like Spooker. They were supposed to be afraid of him, at least if Sir Rupert was going to be happy.

Not that he wanted Ben to be frightened. Spooker liked him, and he felt sorry for him.

Spooker sat, thinking.

< 62 >

Maybe, just maybe, he could do the right thing for everyone. He could help Ben out, perform a good haunting on the Ropers, and get good grades from Sir Rupert.

It seemed like a very big job.

< 63 >

CHAPTER 7

By the time morning came, Spooker was asleep.

Huge black dogs with eyes like glowing coals ran through his dreams. They were chasing someone, hunting him down. Spooker wondered who they were after. Then they opened their mouths and Sir Rupert's voice growled, "I'm going to get you, Spooker! You can't escape!"

"I can, I can, I'm really scary!" cried Spooker, waking up in a panic.

"No, you're not," said Ben kindly. He had been sitting at his computer, waiting patiently for Spooker to wake up. "You're not scary at all."

"You don't understand. I've got to haunt your parents," said Spooker. "I have to frighten them, and I mean really frighten them. I've got to do it in two nights or I'll fail my test."

"What test?" asked Ben, confused. "I don't understand what you're talking about. I mean, ghosts usually haunt a place because they died there, don't they? Not because they've got to do some test!" He suddenly stopped. "You, you didn't, did you?"

"Didn't what?" asked Spooker.

"You know, die here," said Ben.

Spooker realized that Ben really didn't have a clue about ghosts.

< 65 >

Spooker began to explain. He told Ben about how you had to go to school to learn how to haunt. He told him about his school, and about the Evil Weed, and his troubles with Sir Rupert.

"The problem is," Spooker said, "he's totally out of touch. He's really old-fashioned, not to mention nasty. But Practical Haunting is really important. If I don't get good grades, I'll fail. I might even have to stay back a year. And I can't stand the thought of his face if that happens. Or the Weed's. Or my parents'. They'd be so disappointed."

"Would they be mad?" asked Ben.

"Not mad. Just sad."

"Mine get mad when I don't do well at school," said Ben sadly.

"They think I'm stupid," he added. "When they think about me at all."

< 66 >

Spooker didn't know what to say. He decided to change the subject. "It's funny that you can see me. Normally, people are only supposed to see us when we want them to."

Ben looked disappointed. "Don't you want me to see you?"

"Oh no, I didn't mean that! I'm glad you can. It's just that when I was doing that stuff in your parents' room, nobody was supposed to see me. I made a mistake. Maybe I wasn't sending out a strong enough signal, or something."

"I think it might be me," said Ben thoughtfully. "I think I've seen ghosts before. My grandmother lives in a house near an old church, and I'm sure I've seen a ghostly monk there."

"Really? Where?" asked Spooker.

< 67 >

"Marksbury Abbey," replied Ben. "It's not far from here."

"No kidding?" said Spooker. "The monk you saw was my Uncle Albert. He's worked at Marksbury for years. He's really good at it."

Ben smiled. "What are you good at?" he asked.

"I'm best at animal hauntings," explained Spooker. "In fact, that's what I've decided to do for the next stage in your parents' haunting. Last night was just a warm-up. Well, more of a freeze-up, really. But tonight will be much better. Tonight, Ben, your mom and dad are going to see . . ."

Spooker paused.

"What? What will they see?" asked Ben, not daring to breathe.

< 68 >

"Something so fearful it will haunt their dreams. Something so terrible it will cast a shadow over every waking hour. Something so—"

"Okay," said Ben, "but what?"

"A ghostly hound, huge and dark, beyond your wildest imagining."

"I can imagine big and dark, no problem," said Ben.

"With eyes as red as the fires of doom," continued Spooker, ignoring him.

"I thought you said you couldn't do scary," said Ben.

"Oh, I'll be able to do this, no problem," said Spooker.

Ben had heard people showing off before. "Okay, then," he said. "Do it!"

"Do what?" asked Spooker.

< 69 >

"Make the dog," said Ben.

"Make it?" said Spooker.

"Yes."

"I don't exactly make it," said Spooker.

"What do you do, then?"

"Well, I turn into it," Spooker said.

"Unreal! How?" asked Ben.

Spooker tried to think how to explain.

"You have to concentrate really, really hard," he said. "You have to gather every bit of energy together. You have to imagine what you want to turn into, sort of make a picture of it in your mind. And you also have to think how the person who's being haunted will feel. That's where I seem to go wrong," he said. "Sir Rupert says the feeling should be terror. But I don't think that's right."

< 70 >

Suddenly, Spooker realized that time was running out.

"Well," he said, "never mind all that. I'd better get started." He looked nervously at Ben. "Are you sure you're okay with this? I mean, it could be, should be, pretty terrifying."

"Don't worry about me," said Ben. "I'm looking forward to it."

Spooker concentrated, putting all his energy into thinking about a giant black hound. Somehow, a different kind of dog kept poking its nose in.

* * *

Spooker opened his eyes and gave himself a little shake. Then he saw his feet. They weren't black, they were golden. They looked much too big for his legs. He had the urge to roll over and slide on the floor and bounce.

< 71 >

Oh no! he thought. Scary ghost hounds don't play!

"Hey, Spooker! Is that really you? This is great! I've always wanted a dog. It'd be nice if you were solid," Ben said, as his hand went right through the dog's body. "But you can't have everything. Come on. Let's go outside."

Part of Spooker knew that he should be thinking about haunting. But a bigger part just wanted to be a puppy.

They crept down the stairs, as quiet as they could, and then they went into the backyard to play.

They played behind the pots and the little shed, and it was more fun than Ben could ever remember having.

They tried to be quiet, but Ben's feet made noise in the gravel, and Spooker kept yapping, like puppies do.

< 72 >

Neither of them saw the figure at the upstairs window.

Mr. Roper was sleeping heavily. He was tired after last night's disturbed sleep. But Mrs. Roper had woken up. She gazed at Ben as he played with a dog that she could only half see.

"Something strange is happening in this house," she said to herself. "I'm seeing things I don't usually see, and I'm feeling things I don't usually feel. I've never seen Ben playing like that before."

The dog seemed to be teasing Ben. It crouched, its tail wagging. Ben circled around it, pretending to pounce. Then suddenly he did. The dog almost seemed to be laughing.

The noise finally woke Mr. Roper up. "What's going on?" he said. "Is there someone outside?"

< 73 >

"It's Ben," said Mrs. Roper.

"Ben? Outside? In the middle of the night?" He rushed over to the window

"Who does that dog belong to?" he said. "What does Ben think he's doing? Look what a mess he's making of the gravel!"

"He's playing, Cyril. He's having fun," said Mrs. Roper.

< 74 >

"He's what? This is too much!"

"I kind of like watching them," said
Mrs. Roper.

But no one heard her. Mr. Roper
stomped off downstairs to put a stop to it.

< 75 >

CHAPTER 8

The next morning at breakfast, Mr. Roper was very grouchy.

"You still haven't explained what you were doing," he said, "playing outside in the middle of the night, Ben. You'll have to rake that gravel this weekend. I want it all neat and tidy again. And where did that dog come from? I've never seen one like that around here before."

"What kind of dog was it, dear?" asked Mrs. Roper.

< 76 >

"It was sort of a mixture, I think. I didn't get a very good look at it," said Mr. Roper. "It seemed to just disappear when I went out into the garden."

"Yes," said Mrs. Roper. "It did just disappear. I was watching from upstairs. It was very odd."

"I think it must have come under the gate," said Ben. "Anyway, I'd better brush my teeth. It's time for school."

He ran upstairs and into his room.

"Psst! Spooker!" he whispered.

Spooker was almost asleep. It had been a very tiring night and he needed his rest. "Yes?" he said.

"I think it's starting to work. I think Mom knows there's something funny going on," said Ben.

< 77 >

"But it's not supposed to be funny. It's supposed to be scary," said Spooker.

"Oh, right. I was forgetting about your test," said Ben. "Hey, it was good though, wasn't it? You were a really great dog. See you later."

After Ben left, Mr. Goole appeared. "Well, this is very interesting, isn't it?"

"Interesting?" asked Spooker.

"Yes. You're beginning to have an effect on the Ropers. Even if it wasn't the one you intended," said Mr. Goole.

"Do you think so?" Spooker was confused. "Neither of the parents seem at all scared."

"Hauntings don't have to be scary, Spooker. You know that."

< 78 >

"Sir Rupert seems to think they do," said Spooker. "According to him, the whole point is to frighten the Ropers so much that I drive them out."

"Those weren't the instructions, remember?" said Mr. Goole. "You're supposed to 'carry out the best haunting you can.' Think about that. Think about what you really want to do in this house. Things are starting to change, and that's because of you."

"Ben's been happier since you came, hasn't he? Haunting doesn't have to be just about scaring people. It can be about making people look at things in a new way. You've started something, Spooker," said Mr. Goole. "All you have to do now is finish it."

* * *

< 79 >

Spooker thought about what Mr. Goole had said. He didn't understand all of it, but he thought it was true about Ben.

It didn't seem as if Ben usually had much fun.

As far as Spooker could tell, the Ropers didn't want their lives disturbed by a messy, noisy child. Ben had learned to keep out of the way. He spent most of his time alone in his room. Spooker couldn't imagine the Ropers having fun with Ben.

In fact, he couldn't imagine them having fun at all.

Spooker couldn't really see what any of this had to do with his Practical Haunting test. Whatever Mr. Goole thought about the future of haunting, it was Sir Rupert who would give him his grade. And Sir Rupert would not be impressed by what he'd done so far.

< 80 >

Which only left tonight. Spooker had to do something that would make both the Ropers realize, without any doubt, that they were being haunted.

* * *

It was already dark when he woke up. Ben wasn't in his room, so Spooker could concentrate.

He tried to remember what they'd done in school. Sir Rupert had taught them ghost stuff based on historical hauntings. Since Buttercup Avenue had no real history, traditional techniques wouldn't help. Then Spooker thought about Poltergeist class. Perhaps that was the answer, some poltergeist activity? Would flying plates and moving furniture be good enough?

The only problem was that he'd never paid much attention in Miss Geist's class.

< 81 >

Suddenly, Spooker noticed that the room was getting brighter. There was a glow coming from one corner of the room. Ah, thought Spooker, more visitors.

A giant black dog, bigger than any normal, earthly dog, appeared in the glow.

Its eyes were red and glaring. Blood dripped from its savage mouth.

< 82 >

"Is that you, Sir Rupert?" asked Spooker politely.

Sir Rupert looked around the room. "I've been keeping an eye on you, Spooker," he snarled, "and I'm not very happy with what I see. No matter what Goole might have told you, you're here to make people frightened. Nice little puppy dogs aren't going to do that, are they? Look at me, Spooker Batt. Look and learn. You've got one night left. Make it count!"

The dog began to grow larger and larger, but the room was too small to hold the huge hound.

"That's the trouble with these new houses," Spooker said.

With a menacing snarl, Sir Rupert faded away. Spooker wondered if the In-specters were to blame for all this attention.

< 83 >

Maybe the teachers were all trying to get out of their way, and that was why he didn't seem to have a minute's peace.

As Spooker's grin faded, he suddenly realized what his real problem was.

It wasn't that he couldn't do it. He didn't even *want* to do it. It was fine to talk about terrifying people when you'd never met them and didn't care about them. But Spooker definitely didn't want to frighten Ben.

Although he didn't much like them, he didn't really want to terrify Ben's parents either. But he had to try, or he'd fail. It was as simple as that.

Ben came in. "Hi, Spooker, you're awake! What are we doing tonight? Is it the scary dog again?"

"No. That didn't work, did it?" said Spooker grumpily.

< 84 >

"Well, they did see it," said Ben. "And it's done something to Mom."

"She keeps smiling, and she asked if I wanted to play any games after school," added Ben. "I didn't, but she looked so eager that I said I would, and we had a great time. Dad asked her if she was feeling okay."

"Oh!" Spooker thought. So Mr. Goole had been right. Things were changing. Change. That reminded him of something. What was it?

It was the story of Scrooge.

"So what's it going to be?" asked Ben.

"Just a minute, I'm thinking," said Spooker. "You enjoyed last night, because it was fun, didn't you?"

"Yes," said Ben, looking puzzled.

< 85 >

"And your mom started laughing and acting like she wants to have fun, too." Spooker pointed out.

"Yes, I suppose so," replied Ben.

"So if your dad learned how to have fun too, then things would really change around here," said Spooker.

"Yes, but you'll never change Dad!"

Spooker now knew what he was going to do for his haunting.

"Don't be so sure," he said. "Stranger things have happened."

< 86 >

CHAPTER 9

Meanwhile, Mrs. Roper was sleeping soundly, but Mr. Roper was not so lucky.

He was restless, so he got up and went into the spare room. But as soon as he went back to sleep, the dreams began again. He couldn't seem to lie still, and he kept muttering things.

"What's going on, Spooker?" asked Ben.

They were crouching together in a corner of the room.

< 87 >

"I'm Dream Weaving. Shh, I've got to concentrate, or he'll stop," said Spooker.

After a while, Mr. Roper grew calmer. Ben thought he could hear sounds, and see dim pictures, like when you look at the beam from a movie projector.

The pictures were moving too fast for Ben to see clearly. There were lots of pictures, flowing around the room and weaving together into a ribbon that wrapped itself around his father's bed.

Mr. Roper woke up. He got out of bed, not noticing Ben or Spooker, and went quietly downstairs. He went into his office and turned on the computer.

Ben couldn't go into the room, because the lights were on and his father would have seen him.

He couldn't see what Mr. Roper was doing, and Spooker wouldn't tell him.

< 88 >

"You'll see in the morning," Spooker said, looking pleased. "Now, I've just got to do some haunting in your mom's room. Then you can show me some more of your computer games."

Spooker wouldn't let Ben watch him as he worked. He wanted it all to be a surprise. So Ben had no idea what he was up to. He didn't hear any bangs or crashes. He assumed Spooker hadn't been throwing furniture around or breaking pots, which was what he thought poltergeists usually did.

Later, they played computer games till Ben was too tired to play any more.

When Ben shut the computer down, he said suddenly, "You said you had three nights for the haunting, didn't you?"

"Yes," said Spooker. "That's right."

< 89 >

"So, this is the last night. You won't go before I wake up, will you?" said Ben.

"No, of course not. I want to see what happens tomorrow," said Spooker. "And even when I do go, I won't be far away. I'll come back and see you."

"Good," said Ben. "It's been nice having someone to be with. Mom and Dad don't like me having people over. They say they work hard and they want peace and quiet when they're at home, not noise."

"I think," said Spooker, "things might change. With a little luck," he added, crossing his fingers.

The next morning, a shout of surprise woke everyone up. Ben rushed into his mother's room.

"Look, Ben, look!" she whispered.

< 90 >

The room was filled with flowers, lilies, tulips, and roses. Bunches of blue and silver balloons with gold ribbon bobbed near the ceiling.

Mr. Roper came in, looking sleepy and puzzled. "Cyril! Did you do this?" asked his wife.

He stared at the flowers. "They're beautiful, aren't they?" he said.

< 91 >

"You never give me flowers! You've always said they're a waste of money! And how did they get here in the middle of the night?" she asked.

"I, I don't know," said Mr. Roper. "But, there's more."

"What? More flowers?" she said.

"No. I mean, more to tell you. I had these dreams. About when I was a child, and my father wouldn't let me play with other children.

"Then there was another dream, an awful dream. Ben was very sick. You are all right, Ben, aren't you? It was a dream, wasn't it?"

"Yes," said Ben. "I'm fine."

"Thank goodness! Then there was another dream." He turned to Mrs. Roper. "You were gone, and I was all alone."

< 92 >

He wiped a tear from his eye. Spooker, who was watching, began to think he'd overdone things a bit. This was getting embarrassing.

"Then I woke up," said Mr. Roper, "and I realized it wasn't too late, so I went downstairs and ordered some things over the Internet."

"You did what?" asked Mrs. Roper, looking confused.

"I don't remember what I ordered, but it seemed good at the time," he said.

"I'll go see," said Ben. He dashed downstairs, switched on the computer, read through some e-mails, and then ran back upstairs.

"Wow!" he said. "You booked a camping vacation, and you've ordered three mountain bikes!"

< 93 >

"And you sent an e-mail to someone who owes a lot of money," added Ben. "You said he could have more time to pay. And you've given lots of money to homeless children. And there was a big note to yourself stuck on front of the computer reminding you to 'Organize Housewarming Party!'"

Mr. Roper fainted.

It was time for Spooker to go. He knew Sir Rupert wouldn't be happy with what he'd done. Ben was, though, so that was something.

Spooker just hoped it would last, and that the Ropers wouldn't slip back into their old ways.

"You made all that happen, didn't you?" asked Ben. "It's amazing! I've never seen my parents like this. What happened to being scary?"

< 94 >

"Don't worry about it," said Spooker. "That's my problem. Now I have to go, or I really will be in trouble."

"All right, but don't forget, you said you'd come back!" said Ben.

As Ben watched, Spooker seemed to slip through an invisible door, and then he was gone.

* * *

"I think it went very well, even if Sir Rupert doesn't see it that way," Spooker finished. He had been explaining to his parents about what happened.

"Well, it sounds wonderful," said his mother. "I love the part about the flowers and the balloons. Mrs. Roper must have been thrilled."

"And weaving dreams! That's very hard stuff. I think you've done a great job!" said his father.

< 95 >

"Anyway," said Mrs. Batt, "Time for bed. Have a good sleep, and then you'll be ready to face Sir Rupert tonight. And remember, we're proud of you no matter what he thinks."

< 96 >

CHAPTER 10

Everyone was talking about their adventures when Spooker got to school that night.

Goof had haunted an old mansion, which had once been the home of a poet called Sir Walter Wessex. He had been in love with Queen Elizabeth I and had written her some quite awful poems.

She got so fed up with him that she had sent him back to his mansion, where he spent the rest of his life, and death, walking up and down the hallways reading poetry.

< 97 >

Goof had enjoyed himself.

"The best part was when a women's tour group came on a bus," he said.

"I did a daytime haunt. I had a copy of Wessex's poems, so I read them to the ladies, and they ate it up! They all rushed off to the gift shop to buy their own copies."

Holly had to haunt a garden that was very overgrown.

"It was so sad," she said. "There was this old lady living in the house the garden belonged to. She was stuck inside because she was in a wheelchair."

"I fixed it so that when she looked out of the window, she saw the garden as it used to be. She was thrilled. I didn't scare anybody," added Holly, "but I don't care."

"So none of us really scared anybody," said Spooker. "I sure didn't."

< 98 >

He was just beginning to tell them about 6 Buttercup Avenue when a loud screech announced the start of school, and it was time for Practical Haunting.

"I suppose you all want to know your grades," said Sir Rupert, smiling nastily.

"Well, tough luck," he said. "Teachers are busy people. You'll have to wait. However, I did visit you all while you were in action. So I do have some remarks to make. You know, when you're a teacher, you always hope that one day you'll come across a student who's truly brilliant."

"Normally you don't," he added. "You're much more likely to come across students who are completely useless!"

A small ghost appeared. Trembling, she said, "Excuse me, sir."

An expression of disbelief crossed Sir Rupert's face.

< 99 >

"Are you interrupting me?" Sir Rupert bent down and said very quietly.

But before he could say any more, the principal appeared. "Is there a problem? I sent a child to tell you that the Chief Inspecter has called a special meeting of the school in the assembly hall. Shall we go?"

< 100 >

Scowling, Sir Rupert marched his class into the assembly hall.

The In-specters were sitting in a row on the stage. The principal went up to sit with them, and the Chief In-specter stood up to speak.

"We are coming to the end of our time here," he said.

< 101 >

He stopped, and frowned over his glasses at the teachers and students.

"Most of the teaching at this school is good. Some of it is outstanding. And some of it—" he paused. It seemed as if he was having trouble finding the right words. "Some of it is absolutely terrible."

All the teachers looked confused.

"To decide how good teachers are at teaching, we In-specters look at how much their students have learned," said the In-specter.

"We kept a very close eye on those students who have been doing their Practical Haunting. This gave us a good chance to see how useful their education has been so far."

< 102 >

"We have been very impressed by what we have seen. The students took a cool, creative approach to the tasks they were given, even when we thought those tasks were far too difficult."

< 103 >

The glance he gave Sir Rupert had icicles in it.

Then the In-specter said, "Those students are marching forward and taking ghosting into the future."

"What's he talking about?" whispered Goof.

"I don't know," whispered Spooker, "but I think we're okay."

"I'd like to single out one special student for the most life-changing piece of haunting we have ever seen," the Chief In-specter went on.

"Spooker Batt, please come forward!"

"What?" said Spooker.

"Who?" asked Sir Rupert.

* * *

< 104 >

After the In-specters left, the principal decided to throw a party.

"I want to thank all of you for your support and hard work," he announced.

"You may have noticed that Sir Rupert Grimsdyke is not with us tonight."

"Sir Rupert has served the Anne Boleyn school loyally for many, many years," added the principal.

"But he has now decided that the time has come for him to move on. He has decided to move to Hollywood, where he feels he has a future in the special effects industry. Until we are able to appoint a new member of staff, his duties will be shared by the other teachers. Now, let the party continue!"

He clapped his hands together.

< 105 >

For a moment, there was a stunned silence from all the students. Then Spooker, with a huge smile on his face, said it for all of them.

"Unreal!"

< 106 >

FAMOUS HAUNTINGS

Some of the ghosts and famous people that Spooker and his friends mention are part of the real history of the British Isles.

Modern eyewitnesses have seen a ghost cat at **King John's** former hunting lodge in Somerset, England. The cat walks through the wall, curls up on the rug, then disappears. The actual King John lived, and hunted, in the 12th Century.

The **White Horse of Uffington** is a giant dirt sculpture carved into the hillside 70 miles west of London. The Horse is over 3000 years old. It stretches 374 feet in length and is 110 feet high.

Sir Walter Wessex is a fictional character. **Queen Elizabeth I**, however, ruled England from 1558 to 1603. She did have lots of writers who wrote poetry for her, and some of it was terrible.

ABOUT THE AUTHOR

When Sue Purkiss was a kid, she loved reading. She loved reading so much, in fact, that she used to get in trouble for doing it too much. Now, she works with young people for half the week and writes during the other half. She was born with six fingers on each hand, and her favorite color is blue.

ABOUT THE ILLUSTRATOR

Lynne Chapman grew up in London, England, and now lives in Sheffield, England, in a big, old house. When she was young, she wanted to grow up to be an English teacher. But she loved to draw so much that she decided to be an illustrator instead. She hates spiders, marzipan, and rude people.

GLOSSARY

In-specter (in-SPEK-tur)—an inspector; one who examines or looks at things carefully

menacing (MEN-uh-sing)—dangerous

panic (PAN-ik)—a strong feeling of fear

poltergeist (POL-ter-geyst)—a ghost that makes noises and throws things through the air

practical (PRAK-tuh-kul)—useful

savage (SAV-uj)—cruel and mean

snarl (SNARL)—a growl

spectral (SPEK-truhl)—ghostly

technique (tek-NEEK)—a method or way of doing something difficult

DISCUSSION QUESTIONS

1. What are your thoughts about ghosts? Talk about your beliefs, your definition of a ghost, and your description of a ghost.

2. What do you think of Spooker's haunting plans? Should he have followed Sir Rupert's directions?

3. The movie "Ghostbusters" was mentioned. What other movies and books does this book remind you of? Discuss and compare.

4. Discuss why the author ended the book with the word "unreal." What other words might fit?

WRITING PROMPTS

1. Imagine that you are a teacher of ghosts. What would you teach and expect of your "ghost" students?

2. This story refers to the story of Scrooge in Charles Dickens's "A Christmas Carol." Review that story, if you are not familiar with it. It is described briefly on page 25. The same sort of thing happens with the Ropers. Write your own story about a character who changes after a ghost visits them.

3. Why did the illustrator draw the ghosts as real people? Draw your own illustration for a favorite page of this story.

INTERNET SITES

Do you want to know more about subjects related to this book? Or are you interested in learning about other topics? Then check out FactHound, a fun, easy way to find Internet sites.

Our investigative staff has already sniffed out great sites for you!

Here's how to use FactHound:

1. Visit *www.facthound.com*

2. Select your grade level.

3. To learn more about subjects related to this book, type in the book's ISBN number: **1598891146**.

4. Click the **Fetch It** button.

FactHound will fetch the best Internet sites for you!